Pizza
on
Saturday

Pizza
on
Saturday

Rachel Anderson

Hodder
Children's
Books

a division of Hodder Headline Limited

First published in Great Britain in 2004
by Hodder Children's Books

10 9 8 7 6 5 4 3 2 1

A Catalogue record for this book is available from the British Library

ISBN 0 340 87402 3

Typeset in Centaur by Avon DataSet Ltd,
Bidford-on-Avon, Warwickshire

Printed and bound in Great Britain by
Bookmarque Ltd, Croydon, Surrey

The paper and board used in this paperback by Hodder Children's Books
are natural recyclable products made from wood grown in sustainable
forests. The manufacturing processes conform to the environmental
regulations of the country of origin.

Hodder Children's Books
a division of Hodder Headline Limited
338 Euston Road
London NW1 3BH

In memory of
Stefen Paul Wharam
1990–2003

I

Friday's Child Is Full Of Woe

What's the worst thing that could ever happen to you?

Falling off a skateboard and snapping your arm in two places?

Tripping over in the dining-hall in front of the whole school and spilling baked beans over Miss Kettle's shoes? (That happened to Jessica who was the droopiest girl in our class. She was so upset that she couldn't stop crying and she had to be sent home. We all knew it should've been Miss Kettle who cried and went home.)

Missing the school fête because you've caught tonsillitis?

Seeing your sports kit flushed down the toilet by one of the bully girls? (That happened to someone I know quite well. She swears she didn't make it up.)

Having a row with your best friend?

Chipping your front tooth by walking into a gate?

Losing your calligraphy pen?

Swallowing a paper-clip?

Finding the dog's been sick under your bed?

When something like any of these happens, maybe you moan a bit, or sulk, or shout. But in the end you get over it because being hurt, and looking silly, and not making too much fuss about any of it, is one of those things you just have to learn if you're ever going to survive growing up.

That's what I believed anyhow. And a year ago, I was such a cleverclogs, I thought I knew everything.

But I didn't know that there's something else that can happen that you don't ever get over but which changes your life forever.

It wasn't one of those things they teach you about, like road safety or playground bullying, to make sure you know how to take care of yourself. So I was totally unprepared and had to work out, as I went along, how to cope (which is not what happens when you accidentally swallow a paper-clip). For the weeks after it happened it was like I was in a storm at sea, buffeted this way and that without control. I didn't cope at all well. I can see it now. Bad sea-traveller, that was me.

It was this time last year, the Friday before half-term. The morning began badly. When I came down, the rest of my family were rushing around the kitchen like crazy chickens.

'Why's everybody rushing about like crazy chickens?' I asked.

'It's *headless* chickens,' Patrick corrected me, checking he'd got the right textbooks before zipping shut his bag.

'Whassat?' I said.

'The usual expression is "headless chickens",' he said and made a clucking noise. Mum was busy boiling me my egg. Soft-boiled. And buttering me my toast. I can hardly bear to remember what a fuss-pot I was about food. Everything had to be just right or I wouldn't eat it.

Dad was making the packed lunches, mine and his. Just as he always did, though perhaps if I think carefully, he was probably in more of a hurry than usual. Patrick and Margaret are loads older than me and they always saw to their own packed lunches.

Dad left mine for me, neatly wrapped in a plastic pack on the kitchen counter beside the bread-bin. He tucked his into his own briefcase. Then he kissed Mum goodbye.

It's a terrible thing to realize. But, on that last morning I ever saw him, I felt relieved when he hurried out to the car. It meant one less person cluttering up the kitchen so I could eat my egg in peace.

I heard him trying to start the car. Eventually, it coughed into life and he drove off to work. Now Mum could concentrate on helping me get ready.

I couldn't find my clean stuff for sports science.

Navy shorts and white shirt. I'm not much good at sport but you have to do it whether you like it or not.

'Mum!' I yelled from the top of the stairs. 'Where's my things?'

'What things?'

'Sports science!'

They weren't in the top drawer where she usually put them.

'What's that you've lost, sweetheart?' Mum came to the bottom of the stairs.

I screamed it again, in a language she'd understand. 'P.E.!'

'All right, lovie. I'll see if I can find them for you,' Mum called back. 'Maybe they're still in the airing cupboard.'

Margaret, my big sister, was hogging the bathroom, slapping on the lipgloss like it was roof sealant. 'Honestly, Charlotte,' she snapped. 'How old are you supposed to be? Can't you ever do *anything* for yourself? How can you bear to let Mum fuss after you all the time?'

'It's not *my* fault,' I replied, all sullen. In those days, Margaret and I were always bickering. I'm the youngest. She's the eldest. Patrick in between. Mum and Dad never fussed over them. They were allowed to do what they liked.

Margaret said, bossy and impatient as though she was a real grownup, 'Anyway, you've loads of other T-shirts. Why can't you wear one of them? When I was your age, I'm sure I knew how to take care of myself.'

'We're not *allowed* to wear any T-shirt we like!' I said crossly. 'It's not like when *you* were there. These days they're much stricter.'

When the new Head had announced how the rules about uniform were going to be tightened up, my friend Alyssa and I had moaned because we wanted the freedom to wear whatever we wanted. The Head said uniform helped towards our confirmation of identity. None of us had a clue what that meant. Miss Kettle had to explain it meant making each of us feel we belonged to the same school.

Margaret said, 'If uniform's so essential, why didn't

you think about it yesterday? Instead of bothering Mum now? She's got plenty else to do.'

What trivial things we used to argue over. But back then, we were a different pair of sisters. I suppose we were in need of a confirmation of identity, to remind us that we belonged to the same family.

Sometimes it can take a person a whole lifetime to discover what real values are. That's what Mrs Wieczerzak thinks anyhow. She says it's only after you've looked death firmly in the face that you can look life in the face. She should know. She's incredibly old and crumpled. She's probably looking death in the face every time she takes a peek in her bathroom mirror.

Even though I was an Upper Junior (still am, but not for much longer), Mum still walked me to school every day. As we reached the gates, I suddenly realized I'd left my 'Earthquakes' folder at home.

'Miss Kettle *told* us to bring them in *today*,' I moaned, as though it was anybody's fault but mine. 'So's she'd have them to mark over the half-term.'

7

At break-time, came another thing to make me cross. I peeped in my lunchbox and gave my sandwiches a sniff like I always do, to see what Dad had put in them. But he'd got them mixed up. His sandwiches were in there instead of mine. He'd been in too much of a rush to check what he was doing.

'Yuurk!' I groaned and snapped shut the lid on the hammy stink.

My friend Alyssa (who is the person whose sports kit was flushed down the toilet by Ruby last term) asked what the matter was.

'Ham and wholegrain mustard,' I said. 'There's no way I can eat this.'

'Perhaps your dad did it on purpose?' Alyssa suggested.

'How d'you mean?'

'Well, as a sort of joke?'

Alyssa's dad didn't live at her home any more so she wasn't to know that a decent dad would never do that kind of thing, not even as a joke.

I said, 'No way. Dad knows. I do not eat meat and I

8

never will, not even if it was the last food left on earth. And nor should anyone else if they have any concern for the world.'

I used to be so firm in my ideas. Once I'd expressed an opinion, I believed it was my duty to stick with it forever. I didn't know that opinions, like people, can shift with time.

At lunch-break, Alyssa offered me some of her crisps. But they were called *Bar-Bee-Kue* which meant they were meat-flavoured even if they didn't have any real meat in them. So I had to refuse. Alyssa crunched them down noisily. I sat beside her and sulked.

'Cheer up, Charlie,' she said. 'I expect you're having one of those blue days.'

'How d'you mean?' I snarled.

'When every single thing goes wrong. Then, tomorrow you'll find everything is brilliant for a whole day.'

I wish it could've been like that. But wishes are for fairy tales, not real life.

'At least it's only small things,' Alyssa went on

cheerfully. She wasn't really trying to console me. She was gloating over the fact that I'd got the mopes and she hadn't.

'It may seem small to *you*, Alyssa Browne, but it's not you who's got nothing to eat except piggymeat and wholegrain mustard, is it?'

'I only meant, at least it's not something *massively* awful like being trapped in an earthquake.'

We'd just finished doing our Earthquake project with Miss Kettle.

I said, in what I thought was a mature voice, 'I consider it would be a most interesting experience to be in an earthquake. How earthquakes happen is a great deal more significant than anything that happens round here. We'd see the ground opening up and swallowing buses and trees falling over sideways.' I was quite cheering myself up at the prospect. 'Don't you think it'd be positively cataclysmic?'

Alyssa's eyes opened wide. I liked using new expressions she hadn't heard before. 'The only trouble is,' I went on, thinking I was impressing her, 'We're not on a fault line so it's very unlikely round here.'

But it wasn't my vocabulary that Alyssa was shocked by. It was the way I was talking.

'Earthquakes aren't a joke,' she said. 'People get *killed* in earthquakes. You don't really think it'd be fun knowing people were trapped under buildings and suffocating to death do you? Because I certainly don't.' Then, as though it was too awful even to think about, she changed the subject. 'Hey, Charlie, it's *Smugglers* tonight. I'm really looking forward to it, aren't you?'

Smugglers was the new youth club we'd both joined.

On Friday afternoon at the end of school, Mum, with Sally on the lead, met me at the gates, same as usual, to walk me home. Mum and Dad hardly let me walk anywhere on my own. Always so protective. 'Better safe than sorry,' they used to say.

It was amazing they didn't put *me* on a lead. I said, 'I bet Sally has more rights than me.' And Mum just laughed.

I *thought* I resented being looked after. But if I'd really wanted more freedom, I'd have done something about it, wouldn't I?

The houses in our street all look the same. Each one, so I considered, was as ugly as the next.

I said, 'If Dad got a promotion, we'd move to a beautiful big house in the country, wouldn't we? With fountains and a flower garden and a paddock.' I didn't necessarily want a paddock because then I'd need a pony to put in it and I wouldn't want the bother of having to take care of a pony, even if I knew how. But it used to be Alyssa's dream to move to the country. And, since we were best friends (most of the time), we shared our dreams.

Then Alyssa thought up a new dream which was to persuade her dad to move back home with her mum. In a way, I'd still got that dream — a mum and a dad living together. Plus a sister, a brother, and a dog. Funny how you don't appreciate the things you've got till too late.

I said, 'I wish our house wasn't so ugly.'

Mum smiled. 'You funny girl. I think it's a lovely home. It may be a bit on the small side. But Dad and I have been here since just after Margaret was born. Compared to the poky flat we used to be in, it seemed like a palace.'

I said, as though moving house was as simple as changing your hair-style, 'I just thought it'd be nice to have a change.'

Why was I so keen on changing things?

Back home, Mum got my tea ready, same as usual, and when Patrick got in from school, same as usual, she put on her green flowery overall with its matching apron, and left for the residential centre where she's a care worker. She did different shifts each day of the week. Friday was a long one because, on Friday nights, most of the other workers wanted to be free to go out.

Meanwhile, Patrick went up to his room to do some revision. He had exams coming up. Our Auntie Maggs called him a brainbox, almost as though she didn't approve of him being clever. But then, she didn't approve of any of us, not even Margaret who'd been named after her.

Margaret had left school as soon as she could. She had a job in an office. On Fridays, she was always off to spend the evening round at her boyfriend's house.

I dressed carefully in my new jeans and purple velvet top. I thought of using some of Margaret's glitter blusher but then I decided it wasn't worth the hassle when she found out. I was quite sneaky in those days. These days, I'm more likely to ask if I want to borrow something and if she says No, that's the end of it, though she's more likely to say, Oh very well, if you must, which is nearly as good as a Yes. I really like it now we get on better. Not all sisters do.

The age-gap between Margaret and me seems to have closed up. Or perhaps there never was a gap and I just imagined it?

I went downstairs (without glitter blusher) to wait for Dad to get back from work and drive me to *Smugglers*.

He never let me walk on my own. He kept saying it wasn't safe for a child of my age. Child? It's true. Back then, I guess I was still a child.

Most Fridays, Dad and I picked up Alyssa on the way.

I waited. I waited some more. Still no Dad. He'd never before kept me hanging around this long. The phone rang. I thought it'd be him to explain he'd been held up but was on his way. It was Alyssa.

'Well?' she demanded. 'Are you giving me a lift or not?'

'Sorry. But my dad's not back yet.'

'Honestly! Mr Unreliable or *what*?' she said and made a rude noise like a blocked waterpipe which was supposed to be an expression of her disgust.

She was rude to me. So I was rude back. I said, 'At least he's not gone off like *some* people's dads.' How *could* I have been so insensitive to poor Alyssa when it wasn't her fault her dad had left?

She said, 'So I suppose he's broken down again?' (She meant my dad's car, not him.) Her dad had a beautiful car, leather seats, the outside all shiny and not a scratch on it. But he didn't often drive her anywhere in it because he wasn't often there.

I said, 'If you're in such a rush, why don't you go on? I'll see you there.'

'All right, I *will!* But you might have bothered to let me know sooner!' she said, and slammed down the phone.

I felt mad at my dad. It wasn't *my* fault Alyssa was going to miss the start of club night. It was his. I thought I didn't like being treated like a small child. But when I wasn't being fussed over, I got annoyed.

I thought, Right, as soon as he gets back I'm telling him: Listen Dad, I'm quite old enough to go places on my own. This is the *last time* I'm letting you drive me *anywhere*.

I wasn't to know there wouldn't be any more last times.

I watched telly with Sally or rather, she lay beside me on the sofa scratching and snuffling while I watched.

After a while, I went and made loads of buttery toast. Then Patrick came down from doing revision.

'Hi Charlie!' he said, surprised. 'You still here? Thought you were off to that club of yours.'

'So did I,' I said. 'Dad's forgot.' Why did I lie? I had no proof he'd forgotten. However, deep down I knew I'd been even ruder to Alyssa than she'd been to me and I needed someone to blame.

Patrick said, 'Must be held up on the ring-road. I'll walk you round if you like? I could do with a break. My head's spinning.' He pretended to unwind his head with both hands and lay it on the table.

'No thanks. Not worth it now.' The truth was, I was starting to have a really great evening, just me and Sally and heaps of buttered toast, not that I was going to admit that to anyone.

Patrick said, 'Oh well, if you're sure?'

'Yup, thanks.'

There was another reason I didn't want Patrick to take me. When Dad finally got in, I wanted to be right here on the sofa, sadly neglected, all dressed up and nowhere to go, so I could pile on the self-pity about him letting me down.

If only it could've worked out that way. But you can't live life backwards. Events happen in their own order and there's no re-arranging them afterwards.

2

Earthquake Day

The sound of Sally woke me. She was whining at the sitting-room door to be let out. It was early morning, pale and pearly. I was still wearing my jeans and velvet top.

'Weird,' I said aloud, and Sally wagged her tail.

I'd been left, all night, to sleep there on the sofa. Nobody had bothered to wake me, take me upstairs, remind me to clean my teeth or tuck me into my bed.

'Lousy family or what?' I said to Sally who put her head on one side as though listening. I had no inkling what was going on. I just knew that not one person in my family had taken any notice of me, all night long.

The light was on in the kitchen. Someone else was up. I padded through and found Patrick. He was fully dressed too. How curious, I thought. He was standing by the sink staring out of the window into the half light. The tap was going drip-drip-drip. I could see the yellow of the street-lamps shimmering just beyond the garden fence. I heard the milk-float whirring by, then a cat yowl. The night had belonged to them, and now it was change-over time.

'Hey, cheep-cheep earlybird!' I said. 'What're you doing?' The tap went on doing its drip-drip thing. He wasn't bothering to turn it off.

'Dad's dead.' He said it in a funny muffled way as though he was a ventriloquist hiding his voice down his sweater. Patrick was a great brother for bizarre jokes. One April Fool's Day, he'd stuck up all the doors with packing tape so none of us could get out. Another time, he'd re-set every clock and watch for an hour ahead. So what kind of joke was this?

I giggled. 'Tee hee, very funny, I *don't* think.'

He mumbled, 'I thought you knew.'

'Know *what*? How can I know anything when I've been asleep?'

Sally began barking, sharp and insistent, by the back door. I let her out quickly so she wouldn't start annoying old Mrs Wieczerzak. There was only a narrow concrete pathway separating our two houses. Occasionally, we could hear her radio playing, and when she dropped things on her kitchen floor, so she could probably hear things that went on in our house.

I wasn't quick enough in letting Sally out. Margaret, too, must have been woken by Sally's barking. She came stumbling into the kitchen in her pink fluffy dressing-gown. She looked gruesome, all blotchy with smeared eye-shadow like a drenched clown's face. She normally took as long removing her make-up as she did putting it on. 'A clean skin,' she used to tell me, 'is the foundation of beauty.'

But last night she can't have been bothered about the foundations of her beauty. I thought, Something strange is going on, and a shiver ran through me. It was like the excitement during a thunderstorm. Another part of me was annoyed that they should have left me sleeping on the sofa. Were they trying to keep me out of whatever was going on? Trying to protect me from the roaring thunder and the electrical lightning?

I said, 'You sure?' What a stupid thing for me to have said. But hearing someone tell you that their dad was dead seemed stupid too, too stupid to be true. I looked at my watch. It was ten past six.

I said, 'Well, if you're making a nice pot of tea, which I'm sure we could all do with, I bet Mum needs some too.' I could hear my voice sounding far off and much too cheerful for this unusual situation. I felt detached from what was happening. It was as if there was a separate me, acting a scene in a play about someone whose father had died.

'Mum's not here,' said Patrick in his choked ventriloquist's way. 'She's at St. Luke's. Where they took Dad. She has to identify him.'

St. Luke's was the hospital the other side of town.

The school secretary had taken me there when I swallowed that paper-clip.

I was about to ask what Patrick meant by having 'to identify' Dad. But Margaret suddenly let out a cry as though she'd nicked herself with a potato-peeler. 'What's going to *happen* to us? I don't want to live without a father. I can't bear it.' Her despair sounded ridiculous, like a toddler who's lost its teddy.

Her sobbing set Patrick off. But not me. I was quite bouncy as I made the tea. Eventually, Patrick blew his nose and managed to drink some. He said, 'There's nothing we can do till Mum's home, so we'd better go back to bed.'

I couldn't sleep. I was still too excited. Wasn't that peculiar? I'd just been given some awful news and it made me tingly with excitement.

Most of Saturday morning passed in an unusual sort of blur. I kept forgetting and having to remind myself, My dad's just died. Each time, I got the same jolt of surprise.

In the afternoon, Mum's sister, Auntie Maggs,

arrived. Normally, she hardly ever comes to visit us.

'It's in times of misfortune that a young widow needs family support,' she announced as she marched in through our front door. Then, she set about organizing us. She completely took over. Mum didn't seem to care. But I did.

'Now then,' she ordered Margaret (who'd had the bad luck to be named after her), 'You will see to the washing-up and Charlotte will lend a hand with plate-wiping and putting away.'

'I don't *usually* dry up,' I protested.

'Just because there's been a tragedy, there's no cause to let the place go to wrack and ruin,' said Auntie Maggs, standing over me to see I dried up properly. She looks like our mum but she isn't one tiny bit like her in character.

'And you, Patrick,' said Auntie Maggs, 'you can tidy up that front room so I'll have somewhere decent to sit in the evening.'

'Why's she got to be here anyway?' I grumbled to Margaret.

'She thinks Mum needs looking after.'

I said to Auntie Maggs, 'Mum's got *us*. We've been looking after her extremely well.' The moment she got back from St. Luke's, Margaret had taken her some scrambled eggs and toast on a tray. Patrick had made her several cups of tea. Later on, I'd fed Sally even though it wasn't normally my job. As I saw it, we could manage perfectly well without Auntie Maggs interfering.

I wanted to ask Mum loads of questions, but she didn't seem to be listening properly and was floating along in a fog, doing whatever Auntie Maggs ordered her to do. I tried asking Mum why Dad had died, but Auntie Maggs interrupted me.

'Ask no questions and you'll be told no lies. Now please let your mother alone to have a bit of peace and quiet.'

'I only wanted to know what happened,' I said, after Auntie Maggs had sent Mum up to bed for another rest.

'Stroke,' said Auntie Maggs shortly. 'Major cerebral stroke.'

I didn't know what that meant. Auntie Maggs didn't seem to be able to explain. She just said, 'The mercy is, he wasn't left like a vegetable,' which wasn't much help. I only found out later that a stroke is when the blood stops getting to your brain so that it's starved of oxygen. It doesn't always kill the person. Quite often they can recover.

Usually, there were people dropping in and out of our house, ugly though it is, all the time. Patrick's friends gathered like chattering starlings by the fence, then clattered up and down the pavement on their skateboards. Mum's friends too used to drop in for tea and gossip all the time. But after Dad died it was like we'd got a contagious disease. Nobody wanted to come near in case they caught it too. The phone rang from time to time, though. Auntie Maggs always tried to get there first.

'It's better if I see to this,' she insisted, pushing me aside. 'I'm more impartial. And enquirers prefer to speak to an adult.'

Our only visitor was old Mrs Wieczerzak from next door. I heard her timid tapping at the back door just as I was about to take the kitchen rubbish out to the wheelie-bin. (Auntie Maggs made me do all the horrible jobs.) Mrs Wieczerzak, whose back was so rounded that her head seemed to grow straight out of her hunched shoulders, was standing on our kitchen step.

'Oh!' I said. 'Mrs Wieczerzak. Hello.' It would have been easier and quicker for her to have gone direct to our front door instead of coming round the back. 'D'you want to come in?' I put the rubbish bag down and stood aside.

'No thank you, dear,' she said in a quavery voice. 'I don't want to disturb any of you just now. But I knew I must pop round to let you know I'm so very sorry to hear your news and if there was anything you thought I could do to help, your mother only has to ask.'

I tried to think of something which wouldn't be too difficult for a bent-up old creature to do. But all of a sudden, there was Auntie Maggs right behind me.

'Thank you for your concern,' she said, tart as stewed apple with no sugar. 'And I shall pass your message on but the family is managing perfectly well.' Then she closed the door so fast that the tip of Sally's tail got caught and made her yelp with pain.

'Mind poor Sally,' I said and deliberately left the rubbish bag on the floor. I heard Mrs Wieczerzak shuffling home on her bandy legs. If you were that ancient, even visiting your neighbour was like a major expedition.

Nobody else came to call and at six o'clock, Auntie Maggs cooked a disgusting tea of macaroni cheese even though I told her we always had pizza on Saturdays.

On Sunday afternoon, Alyssa's mother rang.

'She's asking,' said Auntie Maggs who, of course, took the call before I could get to the telephone, 'if you want to go round to your friend's for a change of scene.'

I thought I did. So Patrick walked me round. But as soon as I arrived at Alyssa's, I felt awful. So I just went on about how awful Auntie Maggs was. Straightaway, Alyssa turned it into a competition to see which of us had the worst relatives. She told me how she'd got *six* awful aunties, each worse than the one before. And I began to realize that I was making Auntie Maggs out to sound much more awful than she really was, just to impress Alyssa and that it wasn't so much Auntie Maggs I minded as the situation that had brought her into our home.

Being round at Alyssa's house, it felt like there really *had* been an earthquake which had left her and me stranded on opposite sides of a huge crevasse with no way of hearing each other across the gap. I thought how the last time we'd talked was Friday when she'd phoned up, all cross because of Dad letting us down. And that'd made me cross back at her, and then with my dad too. Now I wished I hadn't been annoyed with anybody, specially not with my dad. I shouldn't have blamed him for something which wasn't his fault.

All the time I was at Alyssa's, I kept thinking, Why does it have to be him? Why not somebody else's dad?

Why not Alyssa's dad who she only saw once a fortnight? Or why not somebody's very old granddad who'd already got Alzheimer's and was half dead already?

But these things were too difficult to say to Alyssa. I felt she wouldn't understand and she might think I was telling her that her own dad was no use.

I was relieved when Patrick turned up, with Sally on the lead, to walk me home. I took myself up to bed early because I couldn't bear to sit in the living-room with Auntie Maggs and watch the programmes she chose and listen to her grunting.

On Monday, something interesting happened. The flowers started to arrive. First, two arrangements of potted plants in baskets were delivered by florist's van. They were for Mum. They had cards attached.

With all our sympathy said one.

Condolences said the other, beside a picture of a white dove.

An hour later the same florist's van came back with three big bouquets of cut flowers. Mum smiled when I carried them up to show her. But she didn't want me to leave them in the bedroom.

'Take them down and put them in water, there's a dear,' she said.

'What shall I do with them?'

'Put them where everybody can enjoy them.'

So I did as she asked even though I felt I wanted to crawl up on to her lap and sit there like a very small girl.

While I was unwrapping the bouquets I found that one of them had the wrong sort of card with it.

Congratulations and All the Best for Tuesday! it read.

When Auntie Maggs saw it, she was furious. 'It's a disgrace! It's outrageous!' she said and phoned the florist's shop at once to tell them off as though making a simple mistake with a card was the worst sin in the world.

Towards the end of the afternoon, two wreaths arrived. Auntie Maggs was furious about those too.

'Funeral tributes should go directly to the undertaker's or to the chapel,' she snapped, by now more like ice than stewed apple. 'Everybody knows that.'

She always knew exactly what had to be done. And even if she didn't, she made it seem as if she was the expert.

I didn't want the wreaths to be sent away. I liked having all these flowers in our living room. They smelled so fragrant, specially the lilies.

'Hey! We could open our own florist's shop!' I said, jokingly. Auntie Maggs gave me a disapproving look, colder than ice, sharper than sugarless apples. It was in my nature to make light-hearted remarks like that even if I didn't necessarily mean them. They popped out of my mouth like Easter chicks hatching. I'd always been like that. Why did it have to be different now? But Auntie Maggs made it seem like bad manners that I wasn't behaving in a more downcast way.

I overheard her talking to Mum about me. 'Your poor Charlotte,' she said. 'I fear the truth just hasn't sunk in. She's living in her own little dream world. But then, a child of that age, she's probably too young to fully comprehend. Probably for the best.'

At the time I thought I 'comprehended' perfectly well. I wasn't to know that I had a long journey ahead.

For the whole for the next week, which was half-term, nothing happened apart from Auntie Maggs's obsessive frenzy of cleaning. Our home may have been ugly but it definitely wasn't dirty, so why did she have to do so much cleaning?

'My half-term's supposed to be a holiday, a whirlwind of relaxation and excitation,' I grumbled when she put me to dust the banisters.

That was something Dad used to say. He'd come home from work, stand in the hall, sniff the air, and say, 'Aha, do I detect the whirlwind of relaxation and excitation?' Then he'd take off his coat and say, 'How's half-term been treating you so far?' And, more often than not, he'd have plotted some surprise outing for the weekend. One Sunday, he'd hired a narrowboat for the day. Another time it was tickets for a big match.

Then there was a treasure hunt by car. And a jousting display in a medieval castle. And a West Indian-style carnival in a small village. (We got lost on the way but it didn't matter because we got there in the end.) Always something different, always unexpected (to me anyhow).

But now there was no relaxation or excitation, not with Auntie Maggs around. Instead, window-panes were rubbed with a chamois leather, tea-towels boil-washed, cupboards turned out.

'We have to get rid of the weevils,' Auntie Maggs explained.

'We haven't got any weevils,' I said.

'Not now you haven't, my girl,' said Auntie Maggs.

She even managed to make Mum join in. Poor Mum. She was like an obedient little doll, doing whatever she was told to. Every corner of our home was turned upside-down in order to put it to rights. All except the shed in the garden. That was Dad's place. Stacked in the corners were lengths of wood he'd saved, short ends and long planks. On the shelves in tins were salvaged brass hinges, electrical bits and pieces. On the work-bench were his tools.

Nobody meddled in the shed, not even Patrick. And definitely not Auntie Maggs. Luckily, she was too busy finding things to interfere with indoors to have time for Dad's shed.

'Have to keep your mother's mind busy, poor dear,' she said as she got out all the cutlery for Mum for polish. 'Or she'll go to pieces before we even get to the finale.'

She meant the funeral. It was delayed because, when somebody dies unexpectedly without having been ill first, they are not allowed to be buried or cremated straightaway. I didn't know any of this stuff before. Nor did Patrick. But he found out and tried to explain it to me.

'There has to be a *post mortem*,' he said.

'A what?'

'It's Latin. It means "after death". It's a kind of medical examination. They have to find out *why* Dad died.'

I said, 'Auntie Maggs says he died of a stroke brought on by overwork. And she says she saw it coming.'

'Turned into a doctor now, has she?' said Patrick sarcastically. Suddenly, he was in a mood with everybody, me included. He stomped off to the public library on the high street.

I tried to keep out of Auntie Maggs's way so she wouldn't draw me into her mania for housework. No amount of crazy cleaning was going to get rid of my dad.

Mostly, I stayed up in my room with Sally and pretended that she could understand when I talked to her. From time to time she pricked up her ears as though listening out for the sound of Dad. I, too, had an uncanny feeling that he might walk back in at any moment.

3

A Dog's Day

'I've never been to a funeral before.'

Margaret shrugged. 'Don't suppose many girls your age have. I've only been to one. That was Nana's. I can just about remember it.'

I thought of some of those news reports you see on the telly, about wars in faraway places. I said, 'Be different if we lived in a war zone, wouldn't it?'

'What on earth d'you mean?'

'Well, we'd be going to funerals all the time.' I meant,

And then I'd know what to expect because people would be dying all the time, so having funerals would seem more normal.

Margaret gave me an Auntie Maggs-type glance of disapproval. 'Really, Charlie. You do say odd things.'

I said, 'Will we be allowed to cry?'

'Don't see why not, if you want to. That's what a funeral's supposed to be for. The public and formal opportunity to express grief.'

I thought (but amazingly for me back then, had the sense not to say out loud), how *she* wouldn't need to publicly express her grief since she'd been doing so much private grief-expressing lately. Her face was permanently blotchy and her eyes puffy.

I wished I had some grief of my own to express. But I couldn't pretend I had. I still had this absurd idea at the back of my mind that what was happening was some kind of mistake, that Dad wasn't really dead but was going to come back. I guess I can see now that Auntie Maggs was probably right and I *hadn't* fully accepted reality.

Margaret said, 'Come into my room, Charlie, and we'll get ready together.'

She made me wash my hair, then helped me blow-dry it. She let me have a quick squirt with her perfume too, and a turn with her blusher. She didn't usually allow me to touch her things.

'Today's important,' she said. 'We both have to look really smart.'

Part of me wanted to look nice for Dad. He always noticed. 'And how's my gorgeous little sprog today?' he'd say. 'Ooh, we do look fine today. Off to the ball, are we?'

Another part of me knew perfectly well that it didn't make sense. Of course he wouldn't notice me. He wouldn't be there. I said, 'What's the point in dressing up? He won't see.'

'It's not for him. It's so we don't let the family down.' Margaret sounded firm, yet sisterly, without being bossy. I felt a rush of closeness. I put my arms round her and hugged. 'You are truly the most utterly best sister in the world,' I said and Margaret giggled.

'Don't be daft,' she said, pushing me away, but I knew she was pleased. It was good when she didn't think me a pest.

Then Auntie Maggs burst in, without even knocking on Margaret's door, and told me to stop gossiping because we hadn't got all day.

She started ordering Margaret about too, telling her what I was to wear. 'In my opinion, a child her age shouldn't be taken to this event in the first place. But since your mother insists, then her uniform will be the least conspicuous.'

'Oh no, I can't! Not school clothes. That's gross and cruel.'

'It will suffice,' said Auntie Maggs shortly.

The new jeans and purple top were what I considered to be my best clothes. Dad had told me how scrummy they were the first time he saw them. 'I don't care what *you* say,' I said to Auntie Maggs. 'I'm going to wear *these*. And you can't stop me.'

But Margaret whispered in my ear. 'Charlie please, darling. Don't make a scene. Let's keep the peace. Just do as the old bird wants.' For half a second, she sounded like our dad. That's what he used to say. Let's keep the peace.

I relented.

Margaret gave me an approving peck on the cheek and I noticed a whole new pool of tears gathering in her eyes. Just as well they didn't spill out or they'd have ruined her make-up. I just about managed to hold myself back from saying this out loud.

Downstairs, Patrick was trying to be all gruff and male while Auntie Maggs dabbed at his hair with a wet comb.

'Get off!' he said, pushing her away.

She tapped him on the shoulder with the comb, like a warning. 'Now then, young man. You'll have to keep a stiff upper lip if you're to be the head of the family.'

Some of the time I really hated that woman. Cleaning up our house was bad enough. But now trying to force me into school uniform during half-term and trying to tidy Patrick's hair when he was practically grown up was outrageous.

'Right then,' I thought. 'If I've got to wear what the old bird chooses, at least Sally can look good.'

I took her into the kitchen and gave her a quick grooming, then tied a white silk scarf round her collar.

When Auntie Maggs saw she shrieked like a dodo in distress. 'What *does* the girl think she's up to now?'

I remembered what Margaret had said about funerals being the time for expressing grief. If a dog could feel grief, then it had as much right as anybody else to show it.

'I'm getting Sally ready for the funeral,' I said in a special calm voice. 'She is Dad's dog and a full member of this family.'

'You are *not* taking a dog to a chapel of rest. D'you want people to think you're some kind of a heathen?'

My calm voice got lost and a furious voice took its place.

'If Sally's not going, then nor am I!' I shouted. 'That's what you want, isn't it? To leave me behind because you think I'm only a child who doesn't count for anything. A speck of dirt to be cleaned away.'

Just then, Mum came slowly downstairs. She was wearing a dreary grey suit that Auntie Maggs had chosen for her.

When she heard me shouting and saw me stamping my foot, she looked so confused and forlorn that, meekly, I fetched my school coat and quietly put it on.

'Dumb animals do not comprehend mortal grief,' Auntie Maggs hissed in my ear as she shut Sally into the kitchen.

Maybe Sally didn't understand grief but I knew that if Dad had appeared at the front door, she'd have gone berserk with excitement to see him.

As it was, a different man was knocking at our front door, a stranger in a long black coat and black leather gloves. He stood stiffly to attention. His expression was so solemn it looked at though he'd had it pasted on to hide his real face.

'The car awaits,' he said, in such an unnaturally deep

voice that I thought he was putting that on too and started to giggle.

I should've made more of it because it was the last laugh I'd be getting for a long time.

4

What If

Alyssa rang and told me she wanted to come to my dad's funeral. 'I've never been to a funeral before,' she whined, as though she'd missed out on some special outing.

I was not surprised when Auntie Maggs said, No, no and absolutely no.

Afterwards, I was able to reassure Alyssa, 'Don't worry. You haven't missed much.'

It was flat, dull and seemed as if it had nothing to

do with my dad. Halfway through, I began wishing I made Auntie Maggs let Alyssa come too so we could've had a giggle under the pews, just to liven things up.

Nobody cried, not even Mum. She just looked lonely and kept very still, as if she was trapped inside a statue of herself awaiting the prince of her dreams to release her. She was so pale I reckoned she could have done with some of Margaret's blusher on her cheeks.

We sang two hymns which the priest said were the deceased's favourites. I heard Patrick muttering, 'I don't see how that could possibly be,' and I knew he was right. Our dad never went to church. It was Mum who took me to the carol service at Christmastime.

I noticed how loudly Auntie Maggs was singing so I guess the hymns must've been her choice.

The priest spoke about destruction, God Almighty, and life being but a shadow which man walks in. I wasn't sure about any of that then and I'm even less sure now. But I did know that Dad believed that when you were gone you were gone. That was it. End of your existence. I'd heard him talking with Patrick when

Patrick had to write an essay on World Belief Systems.

I hoped Dad was wrong when he'd said how he believed it would be All Over once you were dead. I wanted so much to imagine him floating overhead near the ceiling, and to think of him being so surprised to discover that there *was* an afterlife after all. I wanted to think of him hovering in the seats just behind us, transparent, and watching us thinking of him.

I didn't convince myself.

After the priest's address, a man in a big shiny grey suit stood up and made a speech about what a solid and reliable friend and colleague Dad had been and how they would all miss him. At first, I felt this was a really nice thing to say but, later on, I thought that he was probably making it all up. *I'd* never even heard of this friend and colleague and if he'd *really* been such a close pal, surely we'd have heard of him before.

Nobody stood up during the service to proclaim what a lovely and reliable father of three children the deceased had been.

I nudged Margaret and whispered, 'Don't you think one of us better stand up now and say something about our dad? You know, about how nice he is?'

Margaret looked at me as if she was a person underwater, drowning, and I remembered how, up in her bedroom, I'd promised her that I'd not make any kind of silly scene or exhibition of myself. I had the feeling that, on a day as important as this, a promise was like a solemn vow and had to be kept.

There was more praying, then it was over. The coffin slid backwards on a slow-moving escalator behind some curtains and we trooped into a reception room to be served weak white tea and tough white sandwiches. The sandwiches all had ham in them, every single one. The undertaker's caterer can't have ever heard of vegetarians.

As we left some of the people shook Mum's hand, and two of them patted me on the head, reminding me of how I sometimes felt I was treated like a dog. Then we went home, not in the sleek limousine, just in an ordinary taxi. And because the driver had picked us up from the crematorium he knew what we'd been doing so he didn't try to make any cheerful conversation which made the journey home seem even gloomier.

'That's it, then. Nothing more to be done,' said Auntie Maggs, wiping the palms of her hands across each other as though an unpleasant job had been completed. 'Better get the kettle on.' She gave me one of her special nods which meant *I* had better put the kettle on.

The next day, she went away. What a relief. I thought it meant we'd get back to normal. But there were still things that were part of Dad's dying that had to be done.

The flowers in the front room faded, then wilted and dropped their petals. They had to be taken out and dumped in the wheelie-bin, though I kept the florist's bright ribbons and bows. They hadn't faded. I hoped they'd stay bright forever. I wanted to decorate my room with them.

Dad's clothes had to be sorted. Margaret and Mum did that together. Mum didn't want to keep them. She said, 'I'd rather remember him as he was in life, than have all his empty clothes hanging in the wardrobe.'

Two women came up from the charity shop to collect them. It was strange and a bit horrible to watch the suits and shirts that he'd once been inside being bundled into black bin-bags and loaded into the boot of a car.

The sad news about our family travelled across the Atlantic. Must have been Auntie Maggs at work. An airmail letter arrived from one of Mum's cousins in Canada. She wrote to send Mum her sympathy. *And if you're ever passing through Vancouver,* she ended, *do drop by.*

'Vancouver? Me, drop by?' said Mum with a huffy laugh as if it was another case of if pigs could fly. And I thought she meant that it was as unlikely as us moving to a house in the country because she wouldn't be able to afford it

'You *could* go, Mum, if you saved up,' I said. 'And it'd be really exciting for you.'

'Course I couldn't. Who'd take care of you?'

'Margaret, maybe?'

Mum sank down on to the sofa and switched on the telly. 'Too tired for gallivanting,' she said.

I said, 'You wouldn't have to walk. You'd fly. And there'd be air stewards looking after you and showing you films and bringing you magazines and nice little meals on trays.'

It was another of Alyssa and my fantasies that we thought were so sophisticated, to go on a long-haul flight. Alyssa had told me that vegetarians have to pre-order their meals with the airline.

'Don't go on about it,' Mum said sharply. 'You heard me. I said I'm too tired to go anywhere!'

I thought, Aren't adults strange that even *thinking* about travel makes them feel exhausted? Her tiredness was contagious. I flopped down beside her, held her hand, and watched telly all evening until bedtime. Not as much fun as flying to Vancouver. Later, I realized I'd missed the point about her reluctance to travel. It wasn't so much that she hadn't the money for a big trip but that she didn't see the point. She was too weary even to want to make the effort.

* * *

'School again tomorrow, Charlie.' Mum tried to make it sound as though school was a treat. I'd had an extra three days off after half-term and now I was dreading going back. Mum said encouraging things, like, 'It'll be all right Charlie, once you're there, you'll see,' and 'Mixing with people your own age again will be fun.'

She made the sandwiches for my packed lunch. But they weren't right. She didn't do them the way Dad used to. She spread them with too much butter and she didn't know about cutting them into funny shapes to give me a surprise.

'D'you want me to take you in?' she asked.

'You mean into the class? Course I don't. We'd be like Little Bo Peep and her sheep.' I giggled. Mum giggled. I suppose we were both trying to reassure each other we were all right.

But I wasn't really all right. The first day back was grim. I felt shy, almost like on my first ever day in Infants. The classroom looked so ordinary, exactly the same as it always had. In here, life had been chugging on as though nothing of stupendous magnitude had happened. Nobody said anything special to me, though during Register, Miss Kettle gave me a syrupy smile. If only she could have explained so the rest of the class would have known why I'd been off. Not saying anything made it seem like Dad didn't matter.

I thought about this later. My dad hadn't died a hero's death fighting for freedom in a war. He hadn't rescued someone from a burning building. He had died a small private death. But I couldn't see that then. I thought it ought to be as important to everybody else in the class as it was to me. I wanted to be the centre of attention.

I thought about announcing it in our NewsDay session. That's when we used to tell the rest of the class about items of local interest. Like going to an away match and watching your team win. (That was Darren.) Or being burgled. (Jack's family.) Or talking about your uncle's collection of Roman coins. (Jessica, who managed to make her uncle and his coins sound stiflingly dull.) One NewsDay, Mandy gave out the news that her guinea pig had died over the weekend. Several boys at the back had tittered. So it was just as well that shyness prevented me saying anything about Dad in NewsDay. It would have felt even worse if anybody had tittered.

Everybody in class must have noticed I'd been off school and now I was back but none of them said anything like, Hello, so you're back. Where've you been? A few stared, then quickly looked away so I suppose they must've known. At break, people seemed to avoid me. Alyssa was the only person who bothered to try and be a bit friendly. And even she got it wrong. She sidled across the playground and nonchalantly offered me some of her crisps.

'It's all right,' she said. 'They're cheese.' So I took a handful.

'Poor poor you,' Alyssa went on. 'I know *just* how you must be feeling because it was like that for me when my dad moved out.'

I said, 'No! It's not like you and your dad. *Your* dad takes you out every other weekend.'

'He doesn't *live* with us any more.'

I thought, At least you know he's alive and you *will* see him again. But I didn't bother to say it. If she thought our dads were missing in the same way, good luck to her.

Alyssa wandered back to Jessica and Mandy on the climbing frame. Several times she called out to me to join them. But I didn't feel I belonged with them any more.

In class, they'd begun working on a new project about the lives of the Ancient Egyptians. The Egyptians embalmed their dead with oils and spices so they could come alive in another world. It made me think about Dad. I didn't think about whether he should have been embalmed. Instead, I thought, What if he hadn't died but was just pretending, so he could go and live with another woman, like Alyssa's dad had?

Then I thought, What if he'd died sooner, when I was still a baby so I wouldn't ever have known him?

Next, I thought, What if he hadn't died on the way home from work but at home over the weekend when we'd been there with him. Could we have saved him?

That lead on to another thought. Suppose it had been Mum instead of Dad? Would that have been better or worse?

'Charlotte, dear. I don't think you heard,' Miss Kettle interrupted me. 'Try and pay attention please or you won't be able to catch up. I've just asked everybody to get into groups for sticking up your friezes.'

As the Egyptian friezes went up on the walls turning our classroom into an Egyptian king's tomb, the what-ifs went on whirling round in my head.

What if it was Mum's turn next? She could fall down the stairs. She could get mortally sick. She could be run over. It could happen in an instant. Then what would I do? I'd have no parent at all. The more I worried about it, the more likely it seemed that some awful fate was about to affect my pale and precious mother.

By break-time I could hardly breathe. The moment I heard the bell go, I rushed to the cloakroom and grabbed my parka off its hook. But I didn't go into the playground. I had to get home. I ran all the way. I had to make sure she was all right.

She wasn't there. The doors were locked, front and back. I saw Sally asleep on her bed in the corner of the kitchen. Some guard dog.

I heard old Mrs Wieczerzak pottering about in her garden. I called through the fence. 'Have you seen my mother?'

'Yes duckie. She's left for work, hasn't she?'

I set off for the residential centre. Mum usually walked rather than took the bus because she said the exercise was good for her. I would have taken the bus only I hadn't got any money on me. It was about three times as far as Smugglers Club. I was absolutely knackered by the time I was trotting up the steps into the entrance hall. I spotted Mum in one of the Day Rooms with another care worker helping the residents with their tea. They were making a joke with a funny old man with a face that looked like crumpled-up paper. Even though he couldn't speak, he was cackling with laughter. Just for a moment, Mum didn't look as despondent as usual. Till she noticed me in the doorway. Then her face changed. She looked anxious and upset.

'Charlotte! In heaven's name, what are *you* doing here?'

'I want to make sure you're all right.'

'You great silly billy. Course I am. But you'll be in big trouble if you don't get yourself back into school in double-quick time.'

She fetched me some small change from her purse in the staff cloakroom and told me to take the bus.

I slid into class halfway through Music. Alyssa gave me a sly glance but Mrs Prior who takes all the classes for Music hardly even noticed I was late.

Next morning when it was time to set out for school, the worry started again that something terrible might happen to Mum. At first, she ignored my moaning that I had a stomach ache (which was true) until suddenly I dashed upstairs and was sick.

The stomach ache went away but I got a headache instead.

'Oh no, Charlotte, honeybunch. Why are you doing

this to me? I can't send you out if you're poorly, can I? Whatever shall I do?'

She filled me a hot water bottle, wrapped it in a woolly hat so it wouldn't burn me and let me lie on the sofa with Sally.

'You *know* I can't stay home with you, darling. I *have* to go to work.' I could tell from her voice that she was pleading with me not to make a fuss. 'The people at the centre rely on me to turn up. They need me there. Quite apart from the fact that we need the money.'

So she left me at home on my own. This had never happened before.

'I'll tell Mrs Wieczerzak you're here. Maybe she'll pop in to make sure you don't get lonely.'

The idea of Mrs Wieczerzak popping anywhere was ludicrous. But, as it turned out, it wasn't loneliness that got me. It was anger. As I lay there clutching the hot water bottle and thinking about Mum looking after the old men at the centre, and about Dad not being here when he should have been, I thought, What *right* did he have to leave us?

He shouldn't have let himself have a cerebral stroke. He should have lived a healthier life. He should have forced himself to stay alive. It was utterly selfish of him to have three children and then abandon us so he could go off and lie peacefully in his coffin.

I seethed with fury. I banged my aching head on the arm of the sofa. I clawed at the cushions. I writhed and sobbed with anger. Sally gazed at me with her big soppy eyes as though she couldn't work out what was going on. That only made me madder.

'Don't look at me like that!' I screamed at her. 'I hate you too! I hate you!'

5

A Baby Elephant

You can't stay angry with a dog for long. Nor with a dead person. But if being dead wasn't Dad's fault, whose was it?

Gradually, it came to me that probably it was mine. On Bad Friday morning all those weeks ago, it was I who had willed something interesting and exciting to happen. Therefore, I must have been responsible for everything that then came about. On that Friday morning, when I'd found out that Dad had given me the wrong sandwiches, I'd been angry. Then when he hadn't turned up in time to drive me and Alyssa to *Smugglers* I was so annoyed I'd vowed that he'd pay for it some day. And now it was too late to change anything. I was stuck forever with the heavy weight of responsibility.

I was so unhappy and confused that I really made myself believe this.

I heard Mrs Wieczerzak mumbling to herself as she came shuffling in through our back door.

'Just popped round to check up on you, duckie,' she said, sitting down on the end of the sofa, then heaving herself up again. 'No, mustn't stop. But oh my, you do look glum. When the wind's in the east you're bound to feel a bit under the weather.'

I said, 'It's nothing to do with the weather.' And then I blurted out to her how I'd caused my dad's death.

'And how would that be?'

'With all my bad thoughts.' And I told her all the things I'd wanted to happen to him.

'Why my poor little duckie-pet,' said Mrs

Wieczerzak, sitting down again, right on my feet and squashing them. 'Course it wasn't your fault. Thinking selfish thoughts may not be a very useful way of passing the time, but thoughts would never kill a person. Not even if you believe in the power of voodoo.'

I wasn't entirely convinced. But it was kind of her to try to cheer me up.

'Now then, henny-penny, why don't you stop your brooding and read your nice storybook, and if you feel a little stronger in half an hour or so, you pop round to my place and we'll have a bowl of soup together.'

I didn't want to have soup with her. I don't even like soup. But I couldn't think how to get out of it. So after a while, I stomped round there. I didn't intend to stay but somehow, after the soup (which was bright red and which Mrs Wieczerzak called borsch and which tasted all right, even though it was mostly made of beetroot which I hate) she got me raking up old wet leaves in her garden. I don't even like gardening.

She asked me to put the leaves in a heap where she makes the compost. 'Takes a year or two with leaves.

They rot so slowly. Household waste's quicker. But being on my own I don't have much to throw out. Looks like the wind's changing. A southerly, that's what we need. Blow the wind southerly. But he never did come back, did he?'

I didn't really know what she was on about. Perhaps she wasn't even talking to me but to someone that only she could see in the video of her mind's eye.

Up till that afternoon when I went round to Mrs Wieczerzak's, the first of many as it turned out, I don't think I'd begun to have any deep thoughts about Dad. It was like there was just self-centred anger, and shock and confusion, swishing around inside me like dirty clothes in the washing-machine. But then, in the evening of the day that I'd been round at Mrs Wieczerzak's eating her bright red soup, something changed. There was something new inside. I found I was full to the brim with tears. Perhaps they'd been there all along. Now, it was time for them to start leaking out.

It started when we were watching a nature

programme together, Mum and me. In the old days, before Earthquake Day, Mum hardly ever used to bother with the telly. She was always busy doing something with Dad. Nowadays, the moment she got in from work she switched on. Or if I was already watching a children's programme, she'd flop down beside me and watch whatever it was, even the cartoons. And she'd stay there till past midnight, not even bothering to change channels.

Margaret put her head round the door to say she was putting a pizza in the microwave and did we want some. Mum shook her head and mumbled that she wasn't hungry and I'd already had some scrambled egg. We hardly ever ate our meals together as a family any more.

Margaret didn't approve of the way Mum sat in front of the telly so much. 'Looks like that TV's turned into your new partner, Mum,' she said. 'You know it's not good for you. You ought to get out and about.'

I didn't like her telling Mum off. Even less, did I like her interrupting my viewing. 'Ssh!' I said. 'We're trying to watch an important programme. It's educational, about the endangered life of elephants.'

I was impressed that, although elephants are vegetarian, eating only grass and leaves, they manage to have such a long life-span. However, in the programme, one of the baby elephants in the wildlife park was unexpectedly found dead. Its slack grey body lay in the dust. The wardens were investigating. Was it poachers, disease, attack by a predator? I wasn't so interested in the investigations. What caught my attention was seeing the way the mother elephant stood over the body, touching it with her trunk, willing it to life.

I stared and stared, transfixed by the image, then the tears that were building up inside me began to trickle out, slowly at first, then gathering speed till they flowed like the washing-machine had a serious leak. Mum hardly even noticed, just gave me an absent-minded pat on the shoulder. It had no feeling in it. The tears went on pouring down my face and I was gasping and hiccoughing for breath.

Margaret came through from the kitchen where she'd been eating microwaved pizza all on her own. 'Charlie,' she said. 'Snap out of it, can't you? It's only an elephant!'

'But it's died,' I sobbed. 'The poor little baby. Doesn't anybody here care about it? It's so sad.'

'Oh for goodness sake!' Margaret said. 'You and Mum between you, you're making this place into a house of gloom. I don't think I can stand it a moment longer.' She stood in the doorway with her half-eaten slice of pizza, as though waiting to see if either of us would react and notice she was there. We didn't. 'Very *well* then,' she said. '*I'm* going round to *Richard's*!'

Mum got up and went slowly upstairs without saying anything, not even 'Goodbye', or her usual reminder of, 'Be careful Margaret. Keep to the main street, won't you?' It was as though Mum couldn't be bothered to concern herself over Margaret's safety any more than she could be bothered to hug me when I was crying.

So Margaret stomped out and I was left alone downstairs with no-one to comfort me, not even Sally. Margaret had taken her round to Richard's.

The baby elephant's body was winched on to a truck and the programme ended. There was an American comedy next. It wasn't very funny. That made me cry too.

Eventually, Patrick came down from his room. He was always up there these days. He had a lot of homework. Or at least he said he did.

He brought me a not very clean tea-towel. 'Wipe your face, there's a good girl,' he said. 'If you cry much more you'll be as dehydrated as a prune. And that won't look very pretty.'

I let him lead me upstairs. He stood over me while I cleaned my teeth as though I was about five years old. Somehow, I didn't mind. I wanted to be treated like a baby. I wanted to be young again.

'Into bed with you now, Charlie. Chickens need their rest.'

'I'm not tired,' I sniffed.

'Maybe not. But your mattress needs you here to hold it down and stop it floating away.' Kind but firm. He sounded like Dad.

I had some horrible dreams that night about me and Margaret getting lost in a safari park. But I must have slept more than I realized because I managed to wake up in time to take myself off to school.

The following evening, something happened which was different from anything so far, something which started well and then became horribly scary and then became almost interesting.

I was trying to think of ways of being helpful. It was Mrs Wieczerzak's idea really. She didn't actually advise me to be helpful but she said, 'It must be hard work for your mother running a family without a husband by her side.' I hadn't really thought of it like that before. So I went out to the back garden to bring in the washing off the line. I remembered how Dad sometimes used to do it when he got in from work if Mum hadn't had time. He didn't say he did it to help Mum. He said that the evening light was special and it gave you an extra chance to appreciate it.

As I unpegged the clean clothes and folded them into the basket, it felt good to be doing one of the same things that Dad used to do. And he was right about the evening sky. It was glowing pink, like a gently smouldering fire.

I glanced over at the shed where Dad used to potter about at weekends. There's a painted sign tacked over the doorway. Patrick made it for him in TDC years ago.

DaD'S woRKs Op it said. The H had fallen off. The door was usually kept closed so that Sally wouldn't go in. Now it was half open, like it used to be when Dad was in there mending things. Perhaps Patrick had been in earlier to look for something.

I could remember how Dad leaned over his workbench whistling. I imagined myself skipping over the concrete stepping stones to the shed, then standing in the doorway to watch him fix the broken toaster, or the ceiling airer, or the leg of a chair. We'd not be speaking. Just him doing and me watching. We had a communication which didn't always need words. After all, he'd known me all my life since before I even had a language to speak.

Now, in the rosy glory sky, I almost felt I could see him back there at his work-bench. I knew it wasn't real, just me remembering something good. I could easily recall him glancing up from the work-bench, turning towards me to smile. But when I tried to think of his face, it was blank. Nothing. Nobody.

I couldn't remember any more what my dad looked like! I'd forgotten his face. In less than three months. I was scared. I was sad. I was ashamed. How could I have forgotten so quickly? I was afraid of losing him. But I also wanted to be happy again. I wondered, did being happy mean having to forget what he was like?

Other things had to get worse before they could get better. Most mornings at school I had a tight headache and the classroom felt stuffy and colourless. The way Miss Kettle droned on was so dreary it made you want to fall asleep. There wasn't any point in me listening. Either I forgot whatever she was on about or else I couldn't understand.

Then one afternoon at Going Home Time, Miss Kettle beckoned to me to stay behind. 'Just for a moment, Charlotte,' she said. 'I won't keep you long.'

I thought it was going to be about the scribbling I'd done all over the back of my workbook. It wasn't. Perhaps she hadn't even noticed the lines of gravestones and the black crows with red eyes I'd been drawing where I should have been doing spellings.

'My dear,' she said. 'I just wanted to have a very quick word.'

I scowled, trying to ward off accusations of scribbling.

'Now, dear, I know you're not getting on too well at the moment and I wondered if there was anything I could do? Would you like to talk about it? To me, or to somebody else in the school? Mrs Prior, for example, is a very understanding person. In private, of course.'

In a way I did want to talk. But at the same time, there weren't any suitable words. And even if there were, Miss Kettle had never been the person I'd want to say private things to. She's too efficient. The way I was feeling was far from efficient. It was as muddled as a ragbag. I'd never be able to say anything properly. So I just said, 'No thank you, Miss Kettle. I'm fine. Can I go now please?'

She half-opened her mouth as if she was about to say something else, perhaps try to persuade me to see Mrs Prior. But then she seemed to stop herself before the words got out. She just nodded and said, 'Very well dear. See you tomorrow.'

On my way home I paused at Mrs Wieczerzak's gate. I don't know why I chose her rather than my class teacher, or the music teacher, Mrs Prior, both of whom knew me much better. Perhaps even then, inside my muddle, I sensed that Mrs Wieczerzak was neutral. She wasn't part of my family. She wasn't part of school. She didn't ask questions all the time. She seemed to know about life without having to do too much talking about it. She just got on with living all alone in her slow yet reliable way.

I peered over her gate. She was doing something to a big wooden tub full of earth. She made a grimace every time she bent over, until she realized I was there, watching.

'Planting,' she said without looking up.

'What?' I said.

'Planting for springtime. Narcissi and tulips.'

She was eighty-eight years old. She was looking forward to *next* year? She believed it was worth planting things even though she might not be there to see them? How weird.

I came in through her gate to watch. She didn't seem to mind. Each bulb was covered in several layers of skin, dry and brown like an old person's. When she'd finished planting her outdoor bulbs, Mrs Wieczerzak nodded at me to follow her indoors. On her kitchen table, spread on a sheet of newspaper, were more bulbs. These ones were covered in a purplish skin, flaky like tissue paper.

'Hyacinths,' she said. 'White, and dark pink, almost red. I like to think of them as Christmas colours. Going to pot them up in bowls, put them in a dark cupboard and they should be flowering by December.

It's always encouraging to see a bit of life in midwinter.'

I watched as she buried her hyacinth bulbs deep in black crumbly earth which she called potting compost. She didn't seem to mind getting her hands dirty.

I glanced at the stuff crammed on to her kitchen dresser. Every shelf was full. There were loads of photos, most of them taken a long time ago, judging by the old-fashioned clothes the people were wearing. Some of the photos had faded to a misty yellow. Also, there were several seaside souvenirs made of shells, dusty now, and a sprig of brown heather stuck to a card, and a china doll's head with a crack down one side.

'It's a bit of a muddle up there, isn't it?' Mrs Wieczerzak said, nodding as though agreeing with herself. 'But they're my memories. That's why I keep them. I look backwards with my knick-knacks and forwards with the flowers.'

She washed her hands at the sink, not very thoroughly. I noticed the black compost still under her nails. Then she lowered herself cautiously into an armchair. The only armchair in the room. I thought I could hear her joints creaking. Or maybe it was the springs of the chair. She said, 'Well, now, have you ever thought of making a memory shelf?'

'How d'you mean?'

'For your father.'

'Mum's put a photo of him in the living-room.'

'Or perhaps you'd prefer a memory box? There's more scope. And it's more private.'

'Dunno. Never thought about it.' I must have seemed so daft. I don't know why she bothered with me.

Her chiming clock struck the hour.

'Aha! Time for the news,' she said. 'You better come back another time. And if you'd like me to, I'll show you what to do.' She switched on her radio with the volume up loud, closed her eyes and settled back to listen.

I wondered if, when I was as old as Mrs Wieczerzak, *I'd* still be interested in what was going on out in the world?

6

The Box Of Treasures

I visited Mrs Wieczerzak again next day after school. She wasn't gardening. She said the north wind had got into her bones and made her back sore. I don't know how.

'But it's a fine day for being indoors,' she said. 'And I've got a few things ready to start you off with your box.'

I had imagined some fabulous-looking container, maybe an ancient carved wooden casket, or a crystal and gold jewellery box. So I was very disappointed when Mrs Wieczerzak handed me an empty cardboard shoe-box which had once held a pair of size 5 blue corduroy bedroom slippers, then showed me a pile of old magazines on her sideboard.

'Making your container look just right is the first step, duckie,' she said. 'You have to decorate it. But not any old picture. They need to be just so, don't they?' She sat me down in front of the pile of magazines with a pair of large, not very sharp scissors which made the cutting-out harder to do neatly. 'See, dearie, you choose some pictures that represent your father's interests, whether it's cars or football.'

I shook my head. 'Not cars. Dad thought cars were a drag, just useful for getting from A to B.'

I chose vegetables and dogs as the theme. I explained to Mrs Wieczerzak how, at weekends, Dad liked gardening and going for walks with Sally. (In fact, he mostly liked mending things but I wasn't sure if a picture of an electric toaster, which was the last thing he ever repaired, was decorative enough for a memory box.)

While I was choosing and snipping (and re-snipping where the blunt scissors had made a mess), Mrs Wieczerzak was busy cooking at her stove. She kept stirring and stirring. It smelled terrible. I hoped it wasn't more soup.

'That's glue, duckie, for your pictures. Flour and water paste. It's how we did it back in the old days. Pop in a clove or a bit of nutmeg and it stops it going mouldy.'

I thought, that's just what the Egyptians did with their pharaohs, preserved them with spices.

Using Mrs Wieczerzak's home-made glue, I stuck coloured vegetables round the outside of the shoebox and dog pictures lining the inside. And all the while, I found myself thinking about him, and the memory of what his face looked like began coming back to me. It was as though he was walking towards me along a flat beach, swirly with mist. The closer he came, the more clearly I could see it was him.

'My, that's coming along a treat,' said Mrs Wieczerzak approvingly. 'That'll be fit to carry some of the most treasured memories there ever were.' She found me a rectangle of white card. 'For the lid, sweetheart. Not that it'll really need a label because you'll always know what's inside. But it'll make it look more finished.'

I couldn't decide whether the card should read, *Dad's Memory Box* or *My Memory Box of Dad*. In the end, I chose *The Memory Box about Dad* and wrote it in my best italic handwriting.

At five minutes to six, I told Mrs Wieczerzak it was time for me to go home. I knew that as soon as her clock struck six she'd need to sit down with the news. I left the Memory Box at her house. I wasn't sure if I was ready yet to take charge of it. Besides, it wasn't finished yet. Now that I understood what it was for, I could get going on the next step myself.

Back home, I started to collect things to go into the box. From the shed, I gathered up a handful of curly wood-shavings off Dad's work-bench. Just smelling them reminded me of Dad. I also took a bent screw-driver and a torn scrap of leftover wallpaper. It was the same pattern as in my bedroom. It was Dad who'd helped me choose it.

I found other things too. Behind the washing-machine, a lonely blue sock of Dad's, missing its partner so it was no longer a pair. A postcard he'd sent us from Oslo when he'd gone off to a conference. The ferry tickets from when we went on holiday to the Isle of Arran. A half-used packet of lettuce seeds.

Margaret said, 'Hey, don't take those seeds! You could plant them and grow some more lettuces.'

'No I couldn't. Look, they're already past their use-by date. They probably wouldn't grow. You have to use fresh seeds for the best crops.'

Mrs Wieczerzak had been telling me quite a few useful facts about gardening. She and her husband used to grow most of their own vegetables. He'd arrived in this country from Poland. He was an air pilot, she told me, very brave, and very handsome.

'Only nineteen he was,' she said. 'He missed his

home and the kind of food he was used to. That's how we got started growing our own. Plenty of beetroot of course. And celeriac too. Very fond of celeriac he was.'

'But you can get that at the supermarket,' I said. 'I've seen it.'

'Yes, dear. Nowadays maybe. But not back then you couldn't. There was a war on. The things you wanted were that scarce.'

I was needing to pop round to Mrs Wieczerzak's quite often because I kept thinking of new things to tuck into the memory box. She'd made a space for it at the bottom of her kitchen dresser, between a china jug which she called a ewer, and her sewing-machine (which was the old-fashioned kind with a handle you have to turn).

'And it can stay there just as long as you wish, dearie,' she said. 'Till you're quite grown up, if that's how you'd like it to be.'

It gave me a warm feeling, knowing that all my reminders of Dad were tucked away in my nextdoor neighbour's house for safe-keeping. It was almost as if a little part of myself were hidden there too.

I don't know why, but I never once wondered *why* Mrs Wieczerzak should have helped me so much and encouraged me to keep popping in. It certainly never occurred to me then that she was unhappy too, in her own way, and liked me being there. I was still far too wrapped up in my own thoughts about me and my own loneliness.

Mrs Wieczerzak's potted hyacinth bulbs were busily growing in the darkness, in the cupboard, under her stairs. She opened the low door to let me poke my head in and see how the pale pointy shoots were beginning to push up through the black compost.

'Soon be ready to bring them out and start them getting used to the light,' she said with a nod of satisfaction. She was really looking forward to the sense of achievement in having got them to flower in time for Christmas.

Christmas! Every year, from when you're about four

years old, you know to start looking forward to it. Every year, as it gets closer to the darkest part of the year, you recognize the signs sooner and understand better than the year before that it's on its way. In town, there's the shops and streets being decorated. At school, there's the decorating the classroom and learning new carols. We'd started a project with Miss Kettle to find out about other religious festivals that were about celebrating light, like the Hindu Diwali and the Jewish Hanukkah.

This would be our first Christmas without Dad. Margaret said to me and Patrick, 'It's going to be tough for Mum. Let's try really hard, shall we, to make it a really good day?'

So Patrick and I went out together and chose a little tree from the greengrocer's in the high street. Patrick went up into the loft and found the box of silver baubles and tinsel and while I decorated the tree, he went and bought crackers, fizzy drink, and some new fairy lights because we couldn't make the old ones work. Margaret went off and bought all the proper

Christmas food, the turkey, the plum pudding and the chestnut stuffing (plus a nut-roast for me). Margaret did most of the grocery shopping those days. When she let Mum do it, it was always pizzas and frozen peas.

We were all prepared to do our best for Mum. But on Christmas Eve, just as Margaret was getting out the cookery books and looking up how long you have to boil a plum pudding, Auntie Maggs rang up.

'Whatever's *happened* to you?' she nagged down the line. 'I've been expecting you all afternoon. Hurry up or you'll miss the last bus.'

I started to explain how Margaret and I had bought the food and how we were already getting the Christmas dinner ready. But Auntie Maggs was insistent. 'No arguing with me, dear. There's no way I'm letting you all stay there moping.'

So we had to go over to her place instead. It turned out that she'd suggested it weeks before, that Mum had agreed, then quite simply forgotten to tell us.

So we put on brave faces and somehow we stumbled through an Auntie Maggs' Christmas, pretending to have a good time and putting up with Auntie Maggs keeping on reminding us how Christmas was a time for being together with your loved ones.

I thought of Mrs Wieczerzak who stayed home every year with no loved ones and yet, somehow, managed to be content. Her husband's family had all died in Poland during World War Two, and she hadn't any relatives of her own.

While we were at Auntie Maggs, I was eager to get back to our own home. Yet once we were there, it felt as though there wasn't a lot in the future worth looking forward to. I certainly couldn't think of any worthwhile New Year's resolutions to make.

Dad's birthday was in the New Year, just after the Christmas holidays were over. He would have been forty-three. I said to Margaret, 'What are we going to do about Dad's birthday?'

She said sharply, 'You can't celebrate a birthday for someone who isn't *there*.'

I know now that she was wrong. You can. And it's called an anniversary.

However, when the anniversary day came, none of us mentioned what special day it was even though we all knew. Afterwards, I wished I'd been strong enough to make something of it, to give Mum some flowers, or make her a card, or do any small thing that said, I know this is a special and sad day for you.

But I didn't.

It's easy to have good ideas after the moment has passed. It's far harder to have them at the right moment.

On the evening when it would've been Dad's birthday supper, if he'd been alive to be there, I know Mum cried. She was upstairs in her bedroom, trying to keep it to herself. But I heard through the wall.

I went over to Mrs Wieczerzak to see how her bulbs were doing and to tuck an old photo that Auntie Maggs had given me of herself as a chubby, grinning bridesmaid at Mum and Dad's wedding into the memory box. Auntie Maggs isn't all bad. If that photo had been taken of me, I'd have destroyed it. Auntie Maggs just said, 'No great beauty, was I? Small wonder I never caught a fellow!'

Mrs Wieczerzak asked me how I was.

I said, 'Not too good. But my auntie says it's high time I gave up being so glum.'

'This grieving, duckie-pet,' she said. 'You got to get through it but you got to do it in your own time. Changes *will* come because change is part of the cycle of life. Just like my bulbs.' (Her hyacinths hadn't come into flower in time for Christmas Day after all. She was disappointed, but patient.)

I said, gloomily, 'I'm not a flower bulb that's got to stick up its growing shoot and blossom.'

'No, dearie. Sorry if I'm doing it wrong. I'm not saying I know how you feel. Course I don't. I was well grown up and married before my Pa was carried off. Anyhow, it'll be different for everyone. And you won't forget anything. But as time goes by, the sadness gets that little bit sweeter.'

I wondered if it would. How could sadness be sweet?

We plodded on, heads down, plod, plod plod, like the cart-horses that Mrs Wieczerzak told me they'd used in her husband's Poland so long ago, instead of tractors.

Every evening, Patrick went straight up to his room with a plate of beans on toast and a pile of revision books, and Margaret went round to her boyfriend's house. (They'd got engaged at New Year. Mum wasn't pleased, said Margaret was too young to know her own mind.)

Every evening, I ate my tea off my knee in front of the telly and the moment I heard Mum coming in from work, I popped round to Mrs Wieczerzak's so I wouldn't have to listen to Mum sighing and complaining.

It was Margaret who thought up the first change for our family. She stomped into the kitchen while I was heating up a slice of cold pizza and said something about what a dreary mess we'd let ourselves get in. I thought she was just trying to be provocative.

'How would *you* know?' I said. 'You're hardly ever here.'

'Well, I am now. And I reckon Dad'd be shocked to see us living like this.'

'Like what?'

'Drowning in misery.'

'Stop fussing. Go back to your precious boyfriend. We're OK.'

'But we hardly ever speak to each other any more. You're always round with old Mrs Thingy nextdoor. Patrick's always upstairs studying and Mum's in front of the telly. We never spend any time having fun like we used to when Dad was alive.'

Margaret had always been bossy. It's because of being the eldest. 'So I've decided,' she went on firmly, as though it had all been fixed, 'that tomorrow I'm cooking a family meal and we'll eat it round the table, like proper humans.'

I shrugged and said nothing. But she obviously really meant it, for the following evening she called to me to go and help set the table. Immediately, I noticed there was something slightly different about our kitchen though I couldn't at first work out what it was. Then I clicked. A small change that made a big difference to an ordinary rectangular room, identical in shape to Mrs Wieczerzak's kitchen next door.

'The table!' I said. 'It's moved!' It used to be in the middle. Mum always sat at the end nearest the cooker, Dad at the other end near the fridge so he could reach for a beer. Margaret usually sat next to Patrick because she used to complain that I fidgeted too much. 'It's in the wrong place!'

Then I thought, No! Not the wrong place. Just a new place. It was now under the window. Margaret must have got Patrick to help her shift it. The kitchen looked larger and airier.

I said, 'Wouldn't Dad be surprised!' There was nowhere for him to sit. It felt strange, sitting round the table, without him at the end. I realized that we hadn't sat down, all together like this for a family meal since before he'd died. I can see now that we were probably too scared to. By sitting down in our usual old places, it would have shown up the gap where Dad should have been. Looking back, I can see how our family has always been like a jigsaw. But a magic one that doesn't have a set way of slotting together. Sometimes the bits fit together easily. Sometimes they don't. Sometimes, bits seem to be missing. Other times, all the parts are there.

I recognized, even then and there, and despite my usual feeling that Margaret was annoyingly bossy, that she'd been quite right that time and it was high time we'd got together again. I recognized too, that she'd put a lot of effort into making it a lovely meal that we could all enjoy. She'd prepared Spaghetti Napolitana with freshly-made sauce, not out of a carton. Patrick told me afterwards that she'd been planning to do a Bolognese till he pointed out that I wouldn't have been able to eat it because of the minced beef. Patrick said, 'I persuaded her to show respect for the vegetarians amongst us.'

There was only one vegetarian, me. So I felt honoured that she considered me worthy of making a change of menu.

After the pasta, there was a fancy salad with all sorts of weird things in it which she said was Italian, then a very English-type apple pie with ice-cream. She hadn't actually baked the pie herself, but she'd taken the trouble to go and buy it from the bakery where they bake their own bread.

I didn't realize it then, but I know now that we can never get back what I thought was the missing piece of our jigsaw which is Dad, to make the family picture exactly as it used to be. Instead, sitting round the table in our new places we were creating a new family shape.

After the apple pie, Margaret made a pot of coffee for her and Mum so I stayed at table and we all got to chat a bit. Not about Dad, but about what we'd been doing that day. It was an effort for Mum to join in but she definitely tried and even managed to tell us a funny anecdote about one of the old fellows at the residential centre. Margaret told us how Sally had started to chase another dog when she took her on her walkies but that the other dog had turned out to be too fierce for our Sally and nearly bit her leg off. Patrick told us he'd seen a spotted woodpecker in the park. I told them all about the forthcoming school trip to the Mendips in the summer term. (I was also dropping a hint to Mum that I'd need money for it.)

I didn't talk about the memory box though. I wasn't ready to tell anybody about that yet.

7

A Girl With Sad Eyes

Two weeks into the spring term, a new girl joined our class. The school secretary, Mrs Paxman, showed her in just after Register. Usually, new pupils start at the beginning of the term, not halfway through the week on a Wednesday. Miss Kettle put her to sit next to me.

'This is Charlotte,' said Miss Kettle. 'She'll take care of you, won't you?'

I shrugged. 'Suppose so. If I have to.' It makes me cringe to remember how unwelcoming I was. I will never ever make that mistake again. After all, I may find myself as the new person in some unknown place one of these days.

'Thank you,' said Miss Kettle, seeming not to notice how I was scowling. 'I'm sure you can be friends. Show her round at break, make her feel at home. Now, eyes to the front everybody, no need to stare, and let's get on.'

I thought, Doesn't Miss Kettle understand I don't need any new friends? Can't she tell I'm having a tough enough time with the old ones? I couldn't see why she was making me take on the responsibility of a new pupil when that was her job.

'We're doing history,' I mumbled to the girl. 'The Victorians. D'you know anything about the Victorians? At least it's better than the Egyptians.' She didn't look as though she heard me. She obviously wasn't listening. Reluctantly, I shoved my book slightly nearer to her and muttered, 'Miss Kettle's quite strict. You'll have to try and look as though you're concentrating. You'll never catch up with what we're doing if you don't try.'

How *could* I have been so bossy?

She nodded and stared down at the page but her eyes didn't look as though they were reading. Her face was a pallid grey and her eyes were dark with shadowy rings under them. Her hands trembled as she held them tightly together on her lap under the desk. She didn't smile. She didn't speak, except to repeat her name to me, so quietly I could hardly catch it.

'Anita.'

There was obviously something wrong with her or she wouldn't have turned up mid-week, mid-term. I wondered, perhaps she'd been excluded from her last school. That would have been quite dramatic, specially if she'd done something really bad.

At break, I showed her where the girls' toilets were but I didn't wait for her to come out. I went off and hung around watching some of the others showing off on the climbing frame.

For goodness' sake, I told myself, she looks old enough to fend for herself. Tough on her that she didn't know anybody here. It was her own fault for getting herself thrown out from wherever she was before. It just didn't occur to me that the reason this girl had turned up out of the blue might be nothing as everyday as having been kicked out of another school. All I was thinking was that since it was probably her fault she was here, she didn't need my sympathy.

I know now why she was there. Perhaps if I'd followed the news programmes as closely as Mrs Wieczerzak did, or even just watched the special kids' news on telly, I might've managed a sort of idea about where this girl had come from. But I wasn't into thinking about other people's lives.

The new girl spent the whole of break leaning against the dining-hall wall staring down at her feet, almost as though afraid to look round. Her brown shoes were brand-new. So was her navy uniform and it was much too big for her. She wasn't just shy. She was all jittery. Some of the bigger boys were playing a game of touchball. When the ball bounced near her, she looked really scared, almost as if she thought the boys were about to attack her.

The teacher on playground duty, Mr Dent, went over and spoke to her. I think he was asking her if she was okay. But she didn't move, even to give a nod to show that she'd heard him. It almost seemed as if she was scared of him too. Why should she be scared of a teacher speaking to her?

At Going Home Time, the school secretary, Mrs Paxman, caught up with me in the corridor.

'Thank you, Charlotte,' she said. 'For keeping an eye on Anita. I knew you'd understand.'

A chilly shiver of guilt ran through me. I wondered if Mrs Paxman would find out that I hadn't been helpful, or understanding, or in the least bit thoughtful. Instead, I'd been really annoyed at the way Miss Kettle had dumped the new girl on me.

'It'll be hard for her, coping with a new school, and a new country as well, though the social worker says she has a moderate command of English already. But she's been living in a camp for far too long.'

'A camp?' I thought of brightly coloured tents and clowns and jugglers. But I knew that I must've got it wrong. It couldn't possibly be that.

'One of those awful places they send them to prior to resettlement. So is she making out all right?'

'Er, well,' I stammered. 'I expect she'll be okay.'

'It's going to be difficult after all the upheavals she's been through,' Mrs Paxman went on. It felt as if she was emphasizing my own failings as a caring person, even though I knew Mrs Paxman didn't do that kind of thing.

'What upheavals?'

'Oh dear, perhaps I shouldn't have said anything. I thought Miss Kettle had explained to you about Anita and her mother?'

'No. Explained what?'

Mrs Paxman went all flustered.

I said, 'She's been kicked out of another school, hasn't she? For doing something bad?'

'Goodness me no! Nothing like that!'

'So what's she done?'

'*She* hasn't done anything. It's, oh, it's a *very* difficult situation. Perhaps I shouldn't tell you all this.'

But then, perhaps because she couldn't bear to keep it to herself, she told me anyhow. How Anita had arrived on an overcrowded plane from a country which, as she called it, was 'severely disrupted by civil unrest'. I hadn't a clue what that meant. So Mrs Paxman sort of explained but I think she was trying to leave out the worst bits so it wouldn't upset me.

But even without the worst bits, a picture slid into my mind of something I'd seen on the telly, or half-seen because I hadn't been that interested. Of a house being set alight, and of people inside rushing to get out. Then there'd been men speaking right at the camera in a foreign language and the voice that was translating told how they'd been woken up in the night and told to leave.

I know now that that's what civil unrest means: frightening people, violence, fighting, killing. And it's often between people of the same country, even from the same villages, being violent against one another.

And I also know that it's usually the people who don't want to be part of the fight and who haven't got bullets and explosives and grenades who get hurt most. Every time I think over it, I almost start to cry. Imagining what it would be like if our neighbours, on the opposite side from Mrs Wieczerzak, suddenly came round with guns and told us to leave our home. Or if Richard joined a band of fighters and Margaret had to go with him.

Mrs Paxman said, 'You could say Anita's one of the lucky ones, because at least she and her mother got away. But who'd want to be stateless? I know I wouldn't.'

I didn't know what stateless was. I do now. It's when a person doesn't belong anywhere. If they had to run away from the country they thought was their home because people were trying to kill them, and they haven't found a new country that'll let them live there and call it their own, that's being stateless.

I hadn't thought asylum seekers were anything to do with me. They might as well have been aliens from outer space for all I cared. Quite often, Margaret used to switch channels if Mum was watching anything she considered upsetting so I suppose I could blame my ignorance on her. But I can't go on expecting everybody else to take responsibility for what goes on inside my own head, can I?

These days, if there's an item on the telly about families caught up in some kind of violent trouble, I make myself see how they're not just moving images of strangers but real, ordinary people like us. And I try to remember that just because they're in a faraway country that I've never even heard of, doesn't make it any easier for them to cope with what's happening.

As for Anita's family, I still don't know much about what happened to them. Had her village been bombed? Had her home been burned to the ground? Had her father or her uncles or her brothers been taken away, simply for being men, or for what they believed in their hearts about God or about the leader of their country? Those aren't things she talks about, not to me, anyhow.

But what I did know, even back then on that

Wednesday afternoon when Mrs Paxman was talking about Anita, was that I hadn't treated her like an equal fellow human being but as a nuisance intruding on my life. I'd totally let her down. I felt a choking sensation, like black smoke, rising up in my throat. I deserved it.

'Thanks, Mrs Paxman,' I said. 'I'll look out for her tomorrow. Got to go now.' I dashed for the school gates. I'd never cried in school and I wasn't going to start now. But I felt bad, really bad. I had my safe reliable home, always the same, to run back to. I had my mum, busy earning a living for her family over at the residential centre. I had Sally, waiting to give me a welcome-home tail-wag.

I had Auntie Maggs. Yes, weird though it may sound, I thought of her too. Okay, I can admit it. I hadn't always been very fond of her. But she was part of my life and it was better to have her than no aunt at all.

She was due to come and stay with us again. She'd offered to help Mum repaint the front room. I wasn't dreading it as much as I thought I would. I was beginning to discover that underneath her bossy manner, she actually had quite a sense of fun. She's got several funny stories to tell about when Dad and Mum first met, and how Dad wanted to ask Mum out but got cold feet and tried to back out of it, so it was Mum who plucked up the courage to ask him out instead. And, maybe (this is my own theory, and quite new, and definitely very private, though I may tell Alyssa about it one day), Auntie Maggs gets grumpy because she never had the good fortune to find someone as terrific as my dad. Mum said recently, 'Even if I'd only known your dad for a week, it would've been worth it.'

I immediately wanted to say, 'But if you'd only known him for a week, you'd never have had *me!*' Then I realized that I was being completely self-centred again. It's better merely to think that kind of thing, and no need to say it aloud.

Sally gave me a tail-wag and a welcome-home lick. Patrick said, 'Hiya, Charlie.'

I said, 'Hello Patrick. You okay?' I was so glad I had a brother who hadn't been rounded up and forced to carry a gun and made to shoot his neighbours.

I poured myself a glass of milk from the fridge and I ate a chocolate finger biscuit from the biscuit tin. I had access to luxury food and drink.

After that, I hurried round to Mrs Wieczerzak's. Her indoor hyacinths had begun to flower but I knew she was still worried about the outdoor ones. She was in her front garden, poking around with her stick under the hedge.

'Looking for the snowdrops,' she said to me. Then, 'Ah, there you are, my dears!' to the earth and I guessed she'd found the first snowdrops. She shuffled over to the wooden tubs she'd planted with bulbs in the autumn.

She inspected the dark compost, checking up on each little yellow snout pushing up to the light, as though it was a newborn baby having its medical.

'Ah, well done,' she said, more to herself than to me, and I knew she was pleased with the progress of her planted dependents.

I said, 'Mrs Wieczerzak, do you think it's time for me to take my box home?'

She nodded without saying anything.

'I mean, Mrs Wieczerzak, I think it might be.'

'That's right, my duckie-pet. Whenever you feel you're ready. And you know, dear, it can always come back here on my shelf and you can go on putting things in for a long time yet.'

So, after I'd admired the earth where the snowdrops would soon be showing and the other damp black earth where tulips and narcissi would bloom in spring, I carried the decorated shoe-box home as gently as if it were full of new-laid eggs. Quickly up the stairs and into my room for I still didn't feel I was yet ready to show it around.

Maybe one day.

Maybe never.

Maybe soon.

I set the box on the chest of drawers. The flower and vegetable cut-outs looked bright and fresh enough, but I saw how some of the paper edges needed another dab of Mrs Wieczerzak's special boiled-up paste to stop them peeling off.

I lifted off the lid. I took out the treasures. The crooked screw-driver, the twist of wood shaving, the lonely blue sock, and all the rest. One by one. And I laid them on my bed. These small things weren't my dad but they helped me think about him. Then I thought about myself. I wondered, If I grew up (of *course* I'll grow up!) will I reach the same age as he'd been? Might I become a parent? Would there be a child, or even a grandchild, who cared enough about me to want to create a memory box? And what might this future child choose to represent me? I didn't add up to much so far.

They'd need to choose pictures of people. Of my family, of course. And of Sally. And also of my friends.

Alyssa, my same-age friend, who I've known since we both started in Reception. Anita, the other, newer, acquaintance who might one day become my friend. And my old friend Mrs Wieczerzak.

I heard Patrick calling up the stairs, 'Charlie! Mum's back. Time for tea.'

I replaced the items carefully. Inside the box there

were no memories of war, no images of houses burning, no newspaper pictures of shootings. Almost every one of my memories was a good one because I am one of the fortunate children of the world.

Perhaps, quite soon, I won't need to keep these memory things hidden inside the box. Perhaps I'll want to bring them out to the light of day and make a memory shelf, just like Mrs Wieczerzak first suggested.

The next day, Anita looked just as pale and shaky. She took a long time hanging up her coat. I waited for her. Perhaps she wanted to run away. But where to? I could tell she didn't want to go into the classroom. I took her hand and led her gently.

At break-time, she dawdled by the desk, fiddled with my pencil-case, putting the pencils all facing the same way. I could tell she didn't want to go out into the playground, noisy with kids rushing about, screeching and shouting.

I said, 'We're not allowed to stay indoors unless it's properly raining. We have to go outside. It's supposed to be good for us. Breathing fresh air or something like that. Stay by me and it'll be okay.' I held her arm steady and lead her over to the climbing frame. I swung myself up on to the lowest bar. Anita followed me, cautiously.

'Shove up, Alyssa,' I said. 'Anita wants to be with us.'

8

As Time Ticks On

I had always suspected that Auntie Maggs was wrong when she'd tried to comfort me by telling me, 'You're young, you'll be over it in no time.' She meant well of course. But I won't ever 'be over it' in the sense of leaving the experience behind. Nor would I want to 'be over it' because that would mean forgetting.

What Mrs Wieczerzak said, even though I didn't understand it at the time, was closer to how it has been. 'A person's age hasn't a lot to do with losing a dear one. When you love someone, it doesn't matter if you are old or young, or if they were old or young. When you're the one who's left behind on earth, it always feels far, far too soon for them to go. It will always feel as though it was yesterday.'

Auntie Maggs also said, in her attempts to offer comfort, 'Everything changes. Nothing stays the same.' At least she was right on that. As time passes, things are changing. It's inevitable. Every day I live is slightly different from the one before. I'm not sure when I began to notice the changes. Of course there's still some sliding backwards into despair which can last for a minute, or a day, or a whole week. But there are the wonderful glory days too when a lovely thought about Dad sails into my mind and instead of hurting, it feels warm and good to be thinking of him.

I've stopped wishing everything last year could have been different. What happened back then is as much part of my life as being born was. It makes me the person that is me.

Soon I'll be finishing junior school and moving on

to secondary. I'm looking forward to it. Patrick will be leaving secondary and moving on to the sixth form college just as I'm arriving. Mum's says it's a pity as he could have kept an eye on me. But I told her that it'll be better this way. I'll have to stand on my own two feet.

Patrick sat his exams but he didn't do very well. In fact, he didn't do at all well. I was surprised. Margaret too. We both thought he'd been revising so hard.

'Heaven only knows what you were doing in your room all that time,' she said.

'Sleeping,' said Patrick. 'For hours and hours. And dreaming. Or trying to dream.'

He'll have to do some re-sits at college. But he's been solidly cheerful about his poor grades. 'Let's keep things in proportion. One student failing history, maths and physics is hardly going to end the world, is it now?'

We had another surprise recently, though I'm not sure if it counts as good or bad. One evening, a man from Dad's office brought his rackety old car back on a low-loader. It had been sitting in the office car park all this time. Since nobody in our family knows how to drive, we hadn't really missed it.

Mr Judd had Dad's raincoat too, also a snap of us which had stood on Dad's desk, and a silly red and green felt calendar which I'd made for Dad when I was still in the Infants. He'd kept it all that time, even though it was long out-of-date. He must have liked having it there to remind him of me, while he was at work.

When Mum saw the old photo with all five of us, plus Sally, on a beach on the Isle of Arran, she burst out laughing. 'D'you remember that day?' she said. 'The wind was so strong we were nearly blown away? Then Dad stepped backwards on to the picnic? It was so funny!'

No, I couldn't remember. But she could and it was lovely to hear her laughing.

I tucked the felt calendar into the memory box. Patrick stuck the photo up on our new kitchen pin-board. He said he'd see if he could get an enlargement made.

The car went on standing, idle, in our driveway until the neighbour who lives opposite asked if we were going to do anything about it. 'Or are you just going to leave it there till it rusts away?' she said in a complaining tone.

'So what *are* we going to do about it?' I asked. Alyssa had complained about it too, saying that if only that old tin heap wasn't always in the way, she and Anita and I could use the forecourt as a roller-skating ramp.

Alyssa and Anita call themselves the two A's. They both come home with me on Fridays. We make our own tea, clear it up, then mess about for a while in the garden. Later, we walk round to *Smugglers*. Anita still doesn't speak much but she seems to like hanging around with us and she smiles more than she used to. Alyssa quite often stops the night at my place. She says that my home has a friendlier feeling than hers. Poor Alyssa. Her parents are still fighting each other whenever they meet.

'The car, Mum!' I reminded her. 'What are we going to *do* about it?'

'Maybe Mum should learn to drive?' was Patrick's suggestion.

Mum shook her head. 'No way! Your dad's the mechanic in this family.' She still sometimes uses the present tense as if he's alive. We know that she knows perfectly well that he isn't. We know it just means that she isn't quite ready to let the past be the past.

'You don't have to be a mechanic to be a driver,' said Patrick reasonably.

I said, 'But it hasn't got its M.O.T. And the licence runs out next month. We can't re-license it till it's passed its M.O.T.'

Patrick gaped at me. Was he even a teeny bit impressed by my new-found knowledge? 'I never knew *you* knew anything about cars, Charlie!' he said.

It's amazing what you can learn by just standing around outside Alyssa's house, waiting for her to get her skates on, and listening to her parents (who have finally decided to get divorced) talking, as reasonably as they can manage, about things like car taxation.

I said, 'It's just a matter of keeping your ears and eyes open.'

Margaret said, 'As a matter of fact, Richard said he'd be happy to tow it down to the garage to get its M.O.T. done. And I've been thinking of taking driving lessons. So maybe we could sign up for lessons at the same time?'

'Ooh yes, that'd be brilliant. Two drivers in the family!'

Patrick said, 'And if you both learned to drive, we could go on holiday back to the Isle of Arran.'

Mum said, 'But it's twelve hours' drive away.'

Patrick said, 'You could take it in turns. And Charlie and I would map-read.'

One slightly sad change happened shortly after the car came back to us. Margaret broke it off with Richard. They're not going out with each other any more.

'We're still good friends,' she insists. But she says they're definitely not planning to get a flat together. Margaret says that she suspects he only asked her to marry him because he felt sorry for her. And she says she only said 'Yes' because she was so upset over Dad that she couldn't see any future for herself. Moving in with Richard seemed an easy way out.

Auntie Maggs says it's just as well because Margaret is far too young to settle down. Patrick says that marriage is an outdated concept.

I said, 'Getting hitched to someone because they pity you doesn't sound like much of a foundation for life.'

Auntie Maggs gave me a warning look. But it's true. Pity is no use to anyone. I'm not ever going to let anyone pity me, not for any reason and specially not because my dad died. I'm going to be proud that I had such a great dad, even if it was only for a short time. I can't say I won't ever get down-hearted again. That would be stupid, when I've still got all this growing-up ahead of me, and turning into a teenager which, so Patrick tells me, is a very hard stage of life.

Alyssa tried to pity me the other day. When I told her about Margaret and Richard splitting up, she kept saying how she was really sorry for me. 'You poor poor thing!' she wailed. 'You must be *so* upset. That means you won't get to be a *bridesmaid*! I know *just* how you're feeling.'

I laughed. If not being a bridesmaid is the worst thing that ever happens to me, then I've got a great life ahead.